FIRE FIGHTERS & FIRE ENGINES

Story by Lisa Peters
Illustrated by Michael Bonner

Previously published as "Firemen and Fire Engines."
Illustrations copyright © 1987 by Price Stern Sloan, Inc.

Published by Price Stern Sloan, Inc.
360 North La Cienega Boulevard, Los Angeles, California 90048

ISBN 0-8431-3289-2

Giant Wonder Books®

PRICE STERN SLOAN
Los Angeles

CLANG! CLANG-CLANG! CLANG-CLANG! A loud alarm sounds in the fire station and tells the fire fighters they must put out a fire. Quickly, they put on their coats and boots and helmets. Some of the fire fighters who are upstairs slide down long poles so that they will not lose any time scurrying onto the fire trucks.

R-R-R-ROOOOOOOOM! R-R-R-ROOOOOOOOM! The huge motors of the shiny red giants are ready to go. Spotty, the Dalmatian, perks up his ears.

The sliding doors roll up. Out of the wide doorway comes the first fire engine, a hook-and-ladder truck. It is such a big truck it needs two drivers. One fire fighter drives in front while the other steers the back wheels.

Next comes the pumper engine. It carries the hose that will be attached to a hydrant. Water from the hydrant will be pumped through the hose and forced high up and far out onto the fire.

An emergency truck rushes to the fire, too. It carries many extra things that the fire fighters may need — extra hose, axes and hooks, life nets for rescue work, first-aid kits, blankets and other things to take care of people.

The fire chief arrives at the fire in a special red car. He hops out and gives orders to the fire fighters, telling them how and where to fight the fire. They obey his instructions.

A high ladder on one of the trucks points up toward the sky. One of the fire fighters climbs to the top of the ladder and shoots a stream of water on the fire.

Others enter the burning building, carrying a long hose from the pumper engine. Some carry axes which may be used to break down locked doors and windows so that the choking smoke will clear away.

At last, the fire is out! The fire fighters have stopped the fire from spreading and burning more of the building. Tired, but knowing that they have done their job well, they return to the trucks.

They ride slowly back through the streets in the hook and ladder truck. They ring their bell gently to let everyone know that the fire is out and that everything is safe again.